FLOWERS
Marta for

Jenn Braddock

Flowers for Marta

The Happy Endings Resort Series, Book 10
Jenn Braddock

Flowers for Marta
(The Happy Endings Resort Series, Book 10)
Copyright © 2015 Jenn Braddock

Cover Design: Kari March (Kari March Designs)
https://www.facebook.com/Karimarchdesigns

Editor: Beyond the Cover Editing
www.beyondthecoverediting.com
https://www.facebook.com/beyondthecoverediting

ISBN-13 Paperback: 978-0692589113
ISBN-10 Paperback: 0692589112

ISBN-13 Ebook: 978-0-9970835-0-7

This book is dedicated to my mom and dad, who have always believed in me in whatever I do. Thank you for your love and encouragement. I couldn't have done this without you.

ACKNOWLEDGEMENTS

I could not have written my first book without the help and encouragement of so many awesome people. I know I'm going to forget people, so please forgive me! You are all in my heart, I promise!

To my BAGGs in FF: Ladies, you reignited my love of reading and writing. I am so thankful for each and every one of you, and my life is so much richer with you in it. I have to give a special shout out to Debbie Kagan, Frances Rosa (my biggest fan!!), Stefanie Pratt, FL Jacob and Rhonda Rivera. You ladies, especially, have been my biggest cheerleaders and sources of encouragement. Thank you for the love, countless pep talks and for believing in me. I couldn't have done this without you!

To my proofreaders/clean readers: Stefanie Pratt, Rhonda Rivera, Susan Gorski, what can I say? You are all rock stars for being there for me on super short notice and helping me to make this a book to be proud of. I cannot thank you enough for your advice, love and support.

To my cover artist: Kari March with Kari March Designs, my cover is absolutely gorgeous! Thank you for working with me on such a tight deadline. Thank you for making this process so easy and worry-free.

Finally, and most importantly, my family. To my parents and sister, who have always loved me and supported all my crazy ideas and careers no matter how far-fetched they seemed. I love you guys more than you'll ever know. To my husband and two beautiful daughters, for listening to my crazy ideas, putting up with my craziness and late nights, and for loving me through it all. I couldn't have done this without you and I love you all to the moon and back.

FLOWERS

Marta for

Chapter 1

From inside the Charleston County Public Library, Marta Dublin paused from reading her newest acquisition from Agatha Christie when the thrum of heavy wheels and the muffled, yet shrill sirens from three fire engines raced by. Two hours later, as the library was closing, Marta stepped out into the damp evening air to walk the ten blocks to her comfortable little apartment above the flower shop where she worked.

This was her daily routine—work at the flower shop until five, walk to the library to get lost in the world of whichever book she happened to be reading at the time, stay until closing, walk home to her two cats, Chloe and Mitzie, and then make herself a light meal before retiring to her bed to read until ten—only to do it all again the next day. Marta was a creature of habit. Her comfortable routine made her feel content.

As she crossed the intersection, faint wisps of smoke rose above the buildings a couple of blocks down. Hurrying toward her apartment, an acrid smell assaulted her senses. Marta's breathing became shallow the closer she got to home. Fire trucks were lined up in front of the building, and fire fighters were extinguishing the last of a fire that appeared to have destroyed her apartment and a large portion of the flower shop where she worked. In shock, she approached a firefighter and tapped him on the arm.

"Sir, that's my apartment. I had two cats in there," she said in her quiet, now tremulous, voice.

"Chief," he spoke into the radio on his shoulder. "I've got the apartment resident here . . . Yes, sir . . . Ma'am, please wait over there. The chief will be right with you." He motioned down the sidewalk a few yards, where Marta's boss, Eloise, stood. Marta's lanky, twig-like legs quickly brought her over to the woman, who stood there wringing her hands.

"Oh, Marta, I am so sorry!" Eloise grasped Marta's hands and pulled her into a hug.

"What happened? How did it start?"

"They're not sure yet. I've been trying to think if we left anything on by accident. A hot glue gun, perhaps? Were there any candles burning?"

Marta shook her head as she tried to think. The fire chief approached them and looked somber as he removed his helmet.

"Mrs. Cranston, this is your shop?"

"Yes sir, it is. I own the building, including the apartment above it. This is Marta Dublin, my employee and renter," she replied, motioning to Marta.

"Ma'am," the chief nodded at Marta. "I hear you had a pet inside the apartment?"

Tears pricked her eyelids as she struggled to find her voice. "Yes sir. Two cats."

"We did a quick search for anyone inside when we arrived on scene, but due to the swift nature of the fire, we had to abandon the search shortly thereafter. I'm sorry, ma'am. We found no cats."

Marta's head dropped and she quickly turned away, trying to hide her tears. Eloise put an arm around her and drew her close to offer what comfort she could.

"The fire appears to have originated in the upstairs apartment, as it has sustained the most damage. Looks to have started inside a wall. Our guess is it was electrical. Mrs. Cranston, we'll be in touch as soon as my report is complete. Meantime, you should contact your insurance company. My condolences to you both."

"Thank you," Eloise replied, shock evident in her voice as she weakly shook the fire chief's hand. He left the two women on the sidewalk together.

"Marta, dear, you'll come stay with LeRoy and me. We'll work something out until we can get everything rebuilt."

Marta choked back a sob as she thought about her two beloved cats and how scared they must have been. She loved them like they were her own children, and the thought of them being left up there to die was just too much to bear. As she tried to regain her composure, she replied hoarsely, "I'll call my sister. I should be able to stay with her."

"Are you sure, dear? I feel terribly responsible for all of this. I want to be sure you'll be all right."

"I'll be fine."

"Well, if for some reason you can't stay with your sister, you'll come and stay with LeRoy and me, you hear?"

"Yes, ma'am," Marta replied, dabbing at her eyes with a tissue she kept at the ready in the pocket of her sweater. Eloise pulled her in for another hug, releasing her when LeRoy approached at a quick pace. As Eloise filled her husband in, Marta stepped aside and reached into her purse for her cell phone. She fumbled over the screen for her sister's number and hesitated before initiating the call.

Marta and her sister, Elaina, had never been what one would call close. They were about as opposite in personality as any two people could be, not to mention Elaina was twelve years her senior. While

Marta was an introvert who saw herself as plain and frumpy, Elaina was confident, pretty and outgoing. Their mother had died during childbirth when Marta was born, leaving her father to raise her and Elaina by himself. He had always favored Elaina, in Marta's eyes. To Marta, her father was a mean man who treated her as nothing more than a disappointment and the reason for the death of his wife. While Elaina had everything handed to her, Marta worked hard for everything she had. Elaina had the best in clothes and shoes, while Marta was reduced to receiving most things secondhand.

Spoiled in her upbringing, Elaina never hesitated to hold her good fortune over Marta's head whenever she got the chance. As soon as Elaina graduated high school and moved away, Marta's existence was solemn and lonely. Her father rarely spent time with her, and she was forced to do most things for herself and him, including laundry, cleaning, and making meals. Her Cinderella life was a sad one. Marta learned quickly that if she stayed plain and quiet and stayed out of the way, her father would all but forget about her, and that was fine with Marta. His silence hurt far less than his attention did. Elaina rarely came home during college and, once she met her husband, William Markham, her visits home became fewer and fewer. William treated Marta no differently than the rest of her family did—not once giving her a chance to prove her worth—and for that, she hated him.

Reluctantly, she dialed her sister's number and waited for her to answer. Just when she was about to give up and take Eloise up on her offer, the call connected and her sister's voice resonated in Marta's ear.

"Maaarta," her sister drawled. "To what do I owe the . . . pleasure?" The pause she took was not lost on Marta.

"Hi, Elaina. How are you?"

"Just dandy. You?"

"Well, to be honest, not very well. My—,"

4

"Marta, I really don't have time to chit-chat. Did you need something?"

Taken aback, Marta paused for a moment. She really didn't want to have to ask for charity from her sister, but she wasn't comfortable staying with LeRoy and Eloise either. Their house was small, barely big enough for the two of them, and LeRoy wasn't in the greatest of health. She didn't want to be a burden.

"Well, my apartment burned down today and I was going to ask if you had a spare room for me to stay in for a while until I can find something else, but I don't want to be a bother."

"Seriously? I swear, you have the worst luck. I guess you can stay here for a little while, but Bill and I are leaving next week for a month's vacation at Happy Endings Resort. I don't think I can have you staying here while we're gone. Bill wouldn't like that."

"Oh, okay," Marta said meekly.

"Don't you have a friend you can stay with?"

"Well, not really. Eloise offered to let me stay with them, but her husband is not doing very well and their house is so small—"

Huffing several times, Elaina finally said, "Fine. You can stay. But I'm not taking your cats. Bill is allergic and—"

"They died in the fire," Marta interrupted quietly.

"Oh. Well that's fine then. You can stay with us until we leave next week."

"I appreciate it, Elaina. I'll be over in a little while."

The line went dead without so much as a goodbye from Elaina, and Marta stared at her cell phone in disbelief. Elaina had not a shred of empathy in her, and Marta knew her sister really didn't care about her. She had no idea what she'd do when they left next week, but that was a bridge she'd have to cross when she got there.

Once she had given the fire chief all of her information, she said goodbye to Eloise and drove to Elaina's house. The house loomed large in front of her as she pulled into their expansive driveway. Marta rang the doorbell and waited quietly. After a few moments,

Elaina answered with a martini in one hand and her cell phone cradled between her ear and her shoulder. She left the door open and wandered away, leaving Marta to wonder whether or not that was an invitation to enter. When her phone call finally ended, she drained her glass and fixed her eyes on Marta.

"So your apartment burned down, huh? How long is it going to take them to fix it?"

"I'm not sure, but probably at least a month, maybe two. It depends on how much structural damage there is to the building. Eloise is hoping to get the flower shop opened up within a month. There wasn't as much damage to the lower half of the building."

Elaina heaved a long sigh as she poured herself another martini from the crystal decanter on the bar. "Well, Bill and I are leaving first thing Monday morning for our month-long vacation. He's out having the RV prepped as we speak. I know he'd never be comfortable letting you stay here without us." Elaina paused mid sip and looked curiously at her sister. "You don't have *any* friends you can stay with?"

Marta knew exactly where this conversation was going to go. She'd had the same conversation with her sister many times, and it always ended up with the same result.

"No, I really don't. I have a few acquaintances, but no one I'd feel comfortable staying with for an extended period of time," she answered.

"If you didn't always have your nose stuck behind the cover of a book or in a bouquet of flowers, maybe you could actually get a *life*! How anyone can be so socially withdrawn is completely beyond me. Daddy was right. You'll never amount to a thing."

No matter how many times she'd heard them, the words still stung.

"Well, there's an empty bedroom on the left at the end of the hall upstairs. Bathroom is across the hall. It's not fixed up or anything. We mainly use it to store crap, but you can use it. I'll find you some bedding."

"Thank you, Elaina," Marta answered.

Elaina disappeared into her master bedroom, leaving Marta standing awkwardly in the hallway. When she returned, she walked to the end of the hall and opened the room Marta would be staying in. Elaina tossed a pile of bedding onto a bare mattress lying on the floor, and kicked a few boxes out of the way before heading for the door again. Marta quietly cleared her throat.

"Elaina? Do you have some pajamas and maybe a toothbrush I could use? I lost everything but the clothes on my back in the fire. I'll go to Goodwill tomorrow to find some clothes, but . . ."

Elaina sighed heavily before stalking out of the room. She returned a few moments later with a flimsy nightgown which she tossed at Marta.

"There are some extra toothbrushes in the closet in the bathroom. Help yourself." Turning on her heel, she left the room once again, closing the door behind her.

Tears streamed down Marta's face. When she had woken up that morning, her life had been as normal as any other day. Now, just hours later, she was homeless, void of any possessions other than her car, and her heart was broken with the loss of her cats. She slowly turned toward her makeshift bed, lifting the pile of sheets and blankets to set them on a dusty box. Slowly, she made her bed with shaky hands, doing her best to stifle her sobs.

Finished, she took the nightgown and walked across the hall to the bathroom. Still shaking, she donned the nightie and looked at herself in the mirror. The generous bodice sagged over her small breasts, and the hem barely reached mid-thigh. She certainly wasn't blessed with a beautiful body like her sister had been. Feeling ridiculous and out of place, she pulled the hair tie from her dishwater blonde hair, letting it fall past her shoulders. Removing her glasses, the mirror reflected her faded blue eyes rimmed in red.

Rummaging briefly through the bathroom closet, she found a toothbrush and a travel-sized tube of toothpaste and proceeded to brush her teeth. When she had finished, knowing she had to cross the hallway in the skimpy nighty, she carefully opened the door. Confirming the hallway was clear, she quickly tiptoed to her room. She heaved a heavy sigh as she leaned against the cool wood of her bedroom door. Trudging over to the bed, she retrieved the Agatha Christie book she had been reading from her worn, yellow, flowered sling bag and crawled into bed. Marta propped her pillow against the wall and leaned back, listening to the crackle of the plastic covering on the library book as she opened the pages so that she could get lost in another world, because her current world was too much to handle.

Marta wasn't sure how long she had been reading when she heard voices coming from down the hall. William was home, and he and Elaina were having a heated discussion in their bedroom. The voices were muffled, but Marta was certain she heard her name mentioned more than once. As stealthily as she could, she pulled back the covers, got up and cracked the door open. The voices were clearer from the hallway, so she opened the door a bit more so that she could hear better.

"You know we're leaving next week, El! You can't fucking expect me to let her stay here while we're gone for a month! She'll either steal shit or we'll come home to a house full of cats. No. Not happening."

"I already told her that, Bill. I asked her if she has any friends she could stay with, but she says she doesn't."

"Now there's a big fucking surprise . . ."

"Bill, be nice. She lost everything she owns, including her cats. She's not my favorite person either, but she's my sister. I can't just put her on the street."

There was a long pause, and Marta figured they had come to a stalemate. She was just about to close the door again when the murmuring began again.

"Bill, just listen to my idea. What if we let her come along with us? She could sleep . . ."

"Are you out of your mind?" Bill's voice was much louder than a murmur now, making Marta cringe. "I'm not going to spend my vacation with that sniveling simp . . ."

"Bill!" Elaina chastised. "Keep your voice down. Just listen to me. She could sleep in the bed space above the cab. Think about it. We'll make her cook and clean, do our laundry . . . we'll have a completely peaceful vacation! She barely ever talks, so I can't imagine that will be a problem. She'll keep to herself when she's not waiting on us hand and foot. Then, when we get back home, with any luck, her apartment will be finished."

After some further mumbling, the knob on their bedroom door rattled. Marta silently closed her own door. She wondered what William's response had been as she heard him stomp downstairs. Deciding that she would deal with whatever would happen in the morning, she returned to her book and, soon after, fell into a fitful, nightmare-ridden sleep, hearing the desperate cries of her kitties as they perished.

Chapter 2

Marta woke early, as she normally did. Opening her bedroom door, the house was still quiet as she padded across the hall to the bathroom carrying her clothes from the day before. She showered quickly and dressed, putting her hair up into a simple ponytail before brushing her teeth with her borrowed toothbrush. Back in her room, she made her bed and placed her meager belongings back into her yellow sling bag. Knowing it was far too early for the Goodwill store to be open, she ventured downstairs to the kitchen, hoping to find something for breakfast.

Marta filled the tea kettle from the stove and turned on the burner, then searched the nearby cabinets for tea and cups. To her left was a coffeemaker, so she held out little hope of finding tea, but she did manage to find an old box of cheap orange spice teabags. She cringed inwardly, but decided it was better than nothing to take the chill off the emptiness in her soul. She detested coffee.

The shrill screech of the tea kettle startled her, and she lunged for it so that the noise wouldn't wake Elaina and Bill too early. She poured the water over the teabag in her cup and cringed at the smell of the tea.

Beggars can't be choosers, I guess.

Opening the fridge to get some milk to kill the taste of the tea, she spotted some English muffins. It took a few minutes of rummaging quietly through the kitchen, but she found the toaster, butter and some honey, which would also improve her tea. In no time, Marta had a simple breakfast prepared for herself. She took a seat on a barstool at the island counter in the kitchen to enjoy her meal in comforting silence. She was just finishing the last of her muffin when Elaina shuffled in.

Elaina's house slippers swooshed against the ceramic tile floor of the kitchen as her silk robe billowed out behind her. Her eyes weren't more than slits and she was mid-yawn when the sound of Marta's teacup on the marble countertop startled her, making her jump. It was all Marta could do not to laugh.

"Shit! You about gave me a heart attack. I forg . . . almost forgot you were here," Elaina snipped. Her slip of the tongue was not lost on Marta.

"I hope you don't mind, I helped myself to some tea and an English muffin. I'm an early riser. I didn't wake you, did I?"

Trying but failing to hide the irritation from her face, Elaina replied, "No, I had set my alarm. I have an appointment at the spa this morning." She scowled. "Where on earth did you find tea in my house?"

"In the back of the cupboard by the stove. I think it's kind of old, but it's fine."

"Good lord, why didn't you just make coffee? The coffee maker is right there," she chastised.

"I don't drink coffee."

Elaina sighed and shook her head on her way to the coffee maker. Soon, it was gurgling and hissing away and the aroma of French roast filled the kitchen. Marta didn't mind the smell of coffee; she just couldn't stomach the taste.

Marta got up from her barstool and brought her dishes to the sink, rinsing them before adding them to the dishwasher. "I'm going to be scarce most of the day. I'm going to check in on Eloise and LeRoy, stop at Goodwill for some clothes, pick up some other necessities and spend some time at the library. You said you're going to a spa?"

"I go every Saturday . . . massage, facial, manicure . . . nothing that would interest you, I'm sure."

"No," Marta paused, "I guess not."

"William and I are having dinner with friends tonight. We'll be late, I'm sure. You can find dinner on your own, right?"

"Sh—sure," Marta stammered, shocked at how self-absorbed and uncaring her sister was toward her. "Well, I'll see you tomorrow then, I guess."

Rather than acknowledge her with an answer, Marta was met with Elaina's back as she began tapping away on her cell phone, completely ignoring the fact that Marta was even in the room.

Lifting her sling bag to her shoulder and with keys in hand, Marta quietly started for the front door. Just as she was passing the staircase, William came bounding down the stairs in linen shorts and a polo, coming up short as he nearly bowled Marta over.

"Shit! Sorry . . . didn't see you. You leaving?" he asked with obvious hope in his voice.

"Just until this evening. Need to find some clothes and other necessities."

"Oh . . . uh . . . we won't be around this—"

"I know," Marta interrupted. "Elaina told me you have plans this evening. I'll be fine. I'll make myself something to eat and spend the night reading in my room."

"Oh. Ok. Well, uh . . . I've got to get to tennis," William mumbled, and he walked to the kitchen.

Once in her car, Marta took a deep breath and blew it out in defeat. *How could Elaina and I come from the same gene pool?*

Over the course of the day, Marta visited with Eloise and LeRoy and helped them sort out all of the insurance paperwork regarding the fire. If the fire truly proved to be accidental with no negligence, the flower shop and apartment would be fully covered and repairs could begin almost immediately. Thankfully, Marta had renter's insurance, so she would likely be able to recoup most of her losses, with the exception of the cats. As she was about to leave their house, the fire chief knocked at the door with the results of the investigation.

"Turns out, it was just as we had suspected. The wiring in the walls was faulty and sparked the fire in the apartment. Building that old, the wiring was bound to be frayed . . . an accident waiting to happen, honestly."

Marta found a few new-to-her outfits at Goodwill for a reasonable price. She thought about the designer clothes that her sister wore, but she wasn't jealous. Marta lived a simple life and she liked it that way. She was smart and could work in higher paying jobs if she wanted to. But being the shy, introverted person she was, she was most content working in a job that made her happy rather than in a high-stress environment, and the flower shop was perfect. She loved her job and was happy to make her modest wage, knowing it was all Eloise could really afford to pay her. It was a small, local floral shop and, in the last few years, Eloise had been finding it hard to compete with the bigger chains and internet sales.

Living a frugal life had its advantages. Living modestly allowed Marta to squirrel away a rather sizeable nest egg so that she would be able to retire comfortably. She was certain that she'd never marry and would only have herself to rely on. She began making wise investments at an early age, and was proud of what she'd been able to save. Shopping at Goodwill and borrowing books rather than buying them was a small price to pay for her future security.

Stowing her shopping bags in her trunk, she drove to the library around mid-afternoon to get lost in the stacks for a few hours. Lost in the pages of a book was Marta's favorite place to be in the whole world. Within those pages, she was safe. She could become anyone she wanted as she became part of the stories.

Before she knew it, her phone chimed six o'clock. The time she went home to feed her cats. An unbearable sadness washed over her as she brushed a few tears from her cheeks. One day, maybe, she'd own another kitty or two. But she just wasn't ready to face that thought yet.

Retrieving her library card, she checked out a couple of new books before heading out to her car. Knowing that Elaina and William would be out for the evening, and not feeling comfortable rummaging through their kitchen for something to eat, she stopped by her favorite Chinese take-out restaurant for some cashew chicken and broccoli, fried rice, and an egg roll. When she pulled up to Elaina's house, she and Bill were just pulling out of their garage.

"Don't wait up, Marta. We'll probably be late," Elaina said after she lowered her window. She was dressed elegantly with diamond teardrop earrings dangling from her ears to match the decadent necklace pressed to her chest, an identical teardrop dangling in the cleavage between her breasts. She looked at Marta's plastic bags and take-out sack with disdain. "Found something for dinner, I see," she muttered.

"Okay, well enjoy your evening. I'm just going to eat my dinner and read. Oh, and would you mind if I used your washer to clean my new clothes?"

Elaina looked at her as though she had just bitten down on a lemon. "*New* clothes?" she scoffed. "I suppose."

"Thank you. Do you have anything that needs washing? I could add it to my load . . ."

"No. That's quite all right. You probably wouldn't know how to wash fine clothes properly anyway. And most of my things go to the cleaners. No, you go ahead. We'll see you in the morning." With that, William sped down the drive, not giving Marta a chance to even reply.

Rolling her eyes, Marta entered the house and set her bags of clothing down near the door. She found plates and a glass in the kitchen and sat down to eat her dinner. When she was finished, she cleared her dishes, put them in the dishwasher, grabbed her bags, and went in search of the washer and dryer. Once the load was started, she wandered back into the large, sunken living room. She looked at all of the expensive paintings, statues and furniture with a scoff of disdain. William and Elaina lived a rather lavish lifestyle. William was the regional manager of a large hotel chain in Charleston, South Carolina and made a considerable salary. Elaina worked part time as a consultant for a trendy makeup designer, also pulling in a pretty hefty wage. Their house and cars and expensive toys were badges of honor for Elaina. They bought only the best, associated with only the upper crust of society, and traveled to the most exotic of places.

However, Marta knew it all came at a price. She knew full well that most of what she saw was a farce. Elaina and William lived *far* beyond their means and were mortgaged and in debt to their eyeballs. If it all came to a crashing halt today, William and Elaina would have to sell everything they owned and they'd probably still owe a hefty sum. Their jobs certainly weren't important enough to afford luxury like this.

She took the Agatha Christie book out of her sling bag and got comfortable on the couch while she waited for her laundry to finish. She was working on the fourth book in the Hercule Poirot series, *The Murder of Roger Ackroyd*. Marta had a list of books and authors she wanted to read during her lifetime, and slowly but surely, she was making a considerable dent in it. She had been a huge Agatha Christie fan ever since she finished *Murder on the Orient Express*, and she had since read more than half a dozen of her books. She had picked up *And Then There Were None* and the Miss Marple series while she had been at the library today, wanting to take a break from Poirot for a while.

When her laundry had finished, she retrieved her bag, book, and clothes and brought them up to her room for the night. She was finishing folding the last of her laundry when she heard a knock at her door, startling her.

"Come in."

Elaina sauntered into the room, looking as if she'd had a bit more to drink than she should have. Her unfocused eyes fell to Marta, kneeling on the floor folding several pairs of new socks. "Get your laundry all done?"

"Yes. Thank you for letting me use your machines. Did you and William have a nice evening?"

Elaina sighed heavily. "Yes, I suppose we did, though some of those women just get to be a bore to listen to."

Marta nodded and turned her attention back to her socks.

"Marta," Elaina began, "William and I have been talking. As I suspected, he is not comfortable letting you stay here for a month while we are gone." Marta sighed resignedly as she closed her eyes, suddenly wondering what she would do. Certainly she couldn't afford to spend a month in a hotel. She had much of her money tied up in retirement investments; nothing liquid enough to last a month paying hotel rates.

"However, if you'd like to come with us to Happy Endings Resort, that would be fine with us." Marta looked at her incredulously, trying not to let on that she'd heard her conversation with Bill the night before.

"Oh, I couldn't let you do that. This is your vacation. I'd just be in the way . . ."

"Nonsense. The RV is definitely big enough for the three of us. You can sleep in the space above the cab . . . maybe help out with some of the cooking or cleaning . . ."

Marta cringed inwardly at that comment. Still, she really had no more appealing options. It might be nice to get away from the city for a while . . . take a vacation of her own. "Are you sure it's okay with William? I don't want to intrude."

"We discussed it last night. I can't just put you out on the street," she commented, looking down at her manicured nails, picking at an invisible flaw in one of them.

"Well, then I accept your offer. Thank you very much, Elaina."

Elaina's head snapped up, looking surprised that Marta had actually consented to join them. "Right. Well, I'll let Bill know. We leave first thing Monday morning," she replied, turning to leave.

"Good night, El," Marta said quietly. Elaina stopped in her tracks, hand on the door handle, but didn't turn around.

"Good night, Marta."

Crawling into her makeshift bed that night, Marta wondered how the next month would play out. She made a mental note to stop at the library the next day to pick up a few extra books to get her through the month. Dozing off, she missed Chloe and Mitzie's gentle purring that used to lull her to sleep every night.

Chapter 3

Early Monday morning, while drinking her favorite tea, something she had been sure to buy after suffering the orange spice, Marta heard a deep horn honking from outside. Elaina squealed loudly from the kitchen and nearly bowled Marta over running to the front door. Marta followed quickly behind and her jaw dropped at the sight. Behind the wheel of a massive, shiny, luxury RV was William, grinning from ear to ear.

"Let's load 'er up, ladies! We've got a vacation to start!"

Within an hour, the RV was packed up and they were on their way. Elaina was riding in the cab with William, and Marta found a plush chair to curl up in and read in the back. A few hours later, they pulled into Happy Endings Resort, winding their way through the campground to find their reserved parking spot.

"I'll go up to the main office and get us checked in, then we can hook up the utilities," William stated as he got out of the RV, stretched, and started his trek to the office.

"Well, what do you think of our home away from home, Marta?" Elaina asked, obviously fishing for a compliment.

"It's very nice. I'm surprised at how much room there is inside. It's a smart design," Marta replied, pushing her glasses up the bridge of her nose.

"Well, I've stocked the pantry with food, and the refrigerator and freezer are full as well. We can shop as we need to." Moving to a tall, skinny door, Elaina opened it with a flourish, looking pointedly at Marta. "All of the cleaning supplies are in here, as well as a hamper where we throw our dirty clothes, towels . . . and the resort has washers and dryers in the cabin just past the office when you need to do laundry."

"Good to know," Marta said, waiting for the other shoe to drop. "I'll be glad to help out when you need a hand," she baited.

"Uh, yeah . . . about that," Elaina scoffed, her face looking like someone had just pinched her. "Bill and I thought it would be nice if you could do the cooking, cleaning, and laundry while we're here. You know . . . earn your keep, so to speak."

And there it was. Just as Marta had overheard the night she arrived at Elaina's house. Resigned to her fate, her shoulders sagged a bit as she replied, "Yeah, sure. No problem."

The two sisters were beside the RV, prepping the hookups when William came back with another man in tow. "El, you remember Edwin," William said, the slightest hint of disdain tainting his pronunciation of the other man's name.

"Of course! Hello, Edwin. How are you?" Marta cringed inwardly at the saccharin dripping from her sister's voice.

"Just fine, thanks. Good to see you folks again," Edwin said quietly. He glanced over Elaina's shoulder, fixing his gaze on Marta with an air of scrutiny.

"Oh, Edwin, this is my baby sister, Marta. She's here with us for the month. Poor thing's apartment caught fire so she's homeless for a while," Elaina said, feigning interest in Marta's plight so she would look like the doting big sister.

Marta rolled her eyes behind her sister's back before stepping forward to shake Edwin's hand, and the eye gesture was not lost on Edwin. He was mildly amused, as he had those feelings every time he had to deal with the Markhams. Still, he approached Marta with caution, assuming she was probably as pampered and privileged as her sister, although she didn't really look it.

"Nice to meet you," Marta said softly, putting her warm hand into Edwin's.

"Likewise," Edwin replied after a beat. "Well, just wanted to make sure everything was all right with your spot and that you're able to get your hookups going."

Edwin was in his early forties. His dark brown eyes hid behind thick-framed glasses and his light brown hair was cut short to minimize his receding hairline.

William and Edwin quickly got everything up and running. With the car unhitched from the rear of the RV, soon Edwin was on his way back to his office. Marta returned inside the RV to decide what to cook for dinner and, after taking a quick inventory of the fridge and pantry, made her decision. She pulled a notebook out of her sling bag and jotted down dinner ideas for the following five days, figuring by then she'd need to go to the store to replenish some of the food items.

A short time later, Marta stepped from the RV, book in hand, in search of a quiet place to read. As she started to wander away, Elaina piped up.

"Where are you headed?"

"Off to read my book."

"What about dinner?" Elaina whined.

"I've got it covered. I'll be back in a couple hours," Marta replied with a touch of smugness as she set off toward the woods.

For the first time in days, a smile crept across Marta's face as she wandered through the tree-lined paths. Everywhere she looked, patches of wildflowers burst from the forest floor in a myriad of colors. Fat, furry bumblebees hovered from flower to flower. Two tiny chipmunks scampered around the base of an elm tree. Before long, she found her own shady oak tree which looked to be the perfect spot. With her back against the trunk of the tree, she stretched her legs out in front of her, pulling the hem of her sundress to just above her knees so that her legs could get a little sun. With a contented sigh, she opened up to where she had left off in the Hercule Poirot series and got lost in the story.

Edwin stepped from his office after spending the last hour paying bills for the resort. Needing to stretch his legs, he decided to take a walk down to the lake to check the ropes tying the rental boats to the docks to make sure they were secure. Two boats had wandered away in the wind last week, and he wasn't looking forward to another rescue mission anytime soon. Nearing the main path to the lake, a movement in the trees caught his eye to his right. Unsure what it was, he edged a little closer. Edwin knew these woods as well as he knew his own name, tending to the trees, flowers and anything else that happened to pop up—or fall down—around the resort. He stopped short and ducked behind a large red pine when he realized what he saw was a guest.

Marta.

From his vantage point, she was resting with her back against a shady oak reading a book. The dappled sunlight glinted on her blonde hair and she wriggled her toes that were poking out into the sunshine. Edwin watched as she turned the page of her book before gently pushing her glasses back up on her nose. As she read, her hand reached out to mindlessly fondle the petals of the wildflowers next to her, and Edwin marveled at her delicate fingers. His heartbeat sped up, and he wasn't sure what it was about her that intrigued him so.

As he shifted his stance, his boot caused a twig to snap, taking Marta's attention from her book. He managed to fully conceal himself behind the tree before she completely turned his way. He stood stock still, holding his breath as he listened to his heart pounding in his ears. Edwin waited a full minute or more before daring to risk a glimpse. When he did, she was back to reading her book and he slowly crept back toward the main path as silently as he could. As far as he could tell, she hadn't seen him, and he scurried toward the lake to check on those boats.

On his way back from the lake, Edwin's mind was on his next task, which was trimming the long grass along the main walkways. He was so lost in thought that he didn't hear anyone coming up behind him.

"Edwin, right?"

Startled, he turned in the direction that the voice had come from. "Uh . . . yeah," he replied, his face turning red and his mind beginning to panic. "Uh . . . uh . . ."

"Marta," she reminded.

"Right. Marta." He nodded and forced a small smile before looking back down at the ground. Edwin was a terribly shy man, especially around the fairer sex. Being the resort manager was a good fit for him, though. He did have to deal with guests and residents, but it was usually them seeking him out. It was much harder for him to initiate conversations. The remainder of his job was taking care of the grounds, which he loved. He enjoyed being out in nature, and he knew a great deal about the native trees, plants and flowers.

"Beautiful day," Marta stated matter-of-factly.

"Uh-huh."

Marta got the distinct impression that Edwin had no desire to talk with her, and was about to turn off on the path that would bring her back to the RV, when she heard him mumble something.

"Pardon?"

Edwin cleared his throat, eyes still downward. "Did you enjoy your book?"

"How did you—" Marta began, then realized she was holding her book in her hand. She chuckled. "Yes, I did enjoy my book. I found a nice oak tree to sit beneath."

Edwin risked a look at her face. Behind her glasses, he could see sparkling crystal blue eyes, and her blonde hair was pulled back at the nape of her neck with a hair tie. Above her left ear, she had placed a tiny, yellow buttercup. She was adorable, and Edwin's heart began to pound.

"That's one of my favorite oak trees. It's quiet there," he said softly.

"It *is* quiet. Wait—you saw me there?"

Edwin blushed again. "Uh . . . yeah, on my way to the lake," he admitted, though he refused to say he had watched her for a while. Now it was Marta's turn to blush. She shifted her book to her other hand and Edwin glanced at the title.

"Hercule Poirot. You like Agatha Christie?"

Marta was surprised. Not many people these days read Agatha Christie, much less knew the characters. "I do. I just finished this one. Next up is *And Then There Were None*. Have you read her?"

Edwin smiled, seemingly forgetting his shyness. "Oh yes. All of her books. I have quite an extensive collection."

Marta beamed. "Wow. I don't run into many people who have a love for Agatha Christie like I do. I've only read half a dozen or so of her books, but I've loved them all. I have to say, I'm kind of hooked. I'd love to see them sometime."

"See who?" Edwin looked puzzled.

"Your collection," Marta replied.

"I see," he said, his shyness returning.

"Well, this where I turn off. I have to go start dinner for their highness," she muttered with an eye roll. "See you later, Edwin."

He nodded and watched her go, wiping his sweaty palms on his dusty blue jeans. He hadn't realized that he was just standing and staring until she looked back over her shoulder and noticed him watching. He turned and continued on his way, his heart feeling a hopefulness it hadn't in a long time.

Chapter 4

Marta soon fell into a routine at the resort. Each morning, she would rise early, make her tea and sit outside the RV in a deck chair reading her book. When she heard Elaina and William stirring inside, she would go start breakfast while she prepped whatever she could for supper. Then she'd clean up any messes they had made and would spend the rest of her day under her favorite tree, reading.

This particular morning, she realized that she was running out of clean clothes, so she gathered up her laundry and asked Elaina for theirs.

"Now, pay special attention to my tops. You cannot put them in the dryer or they'll shrink. And make sure you take my linen shorts out of the dryer immediately, or they'll wrinkle terribly. Oh, and make sure you roll each of Bill's socks for him and put them neatly in his drawer. He's very fussy about them."

It took every ounce of strength for Marta not to roll her eyes at her bossy, pampered sister. It truly made her grateful for the simple life she lived.

Armed with the clothing, detergent, and some hangers, Marta headed for the laundry facility near the main office. She was thankful that she was the only one there. That way, she could do multiple loads at once to save some time. Once she had the washing machines humming, she went outside. She hadn't been around this area of the resort yet, so she took some time to look around. Finding a picnic table situated between the laundry cabin and the main office, she took a seat. It was a gorgeous day with bright sunshine, warm temperatures and a slight breeze. Sitting on the bench facing away from the table, Marta stretched her legs out and leaned her elbows back onto the table. Looking up at the sky, she let her head fall back as she closed her eyes and breathed deeply. She was startled when she felt something furry rub her bare leg.

Looking down, she saw a gray, tabby cat sitting at her feet. Marta smiled and reached her fingers out, letting the feline sniff them. The cat stood back up again, rubbing its cheek against her leg before weaving around and around her ankles. She giggled, reaching down to scratch and pet its head.

"Hey, buddy, where did you come from, huh? What's your name?" she cooed at the cat.

"Sir Henry."

Marta jumped again at the familiar voice coming from behind her. "Oh, you startled me! Good morning, Edwin," she replied, her hand coming to rest over her thudding heart.

Edwin walked around the table, stopping next to her but looking down at Sir Henry. "Good morning," he said softly.

"Sir Henry, huh? Quite the regal name." She smiled and scooted over a bit, motioning for Edwin to sit down. He hesitated for a moment, but took her invitation.

"I have two other cats as well . . . Hercule and Miss Marple. I got Sir Henry and Miss Marple at a local shelter. They think they are brother and sister. Hercule was a stray who decided to make Happy Endings his home. Some of the residents got tired of him begging for food, so I took him in as well."

Marta smiled, realizing that this was the most she'd ever heard this shy man speak in the time that she'd been there. If he was talking about something that interested him, his shyness all but disappeared.

"All named after Agatha Christie characters," she deduced. Edwin smiled and nodded. "Well, he's very handsome."

"I beg your pardon?" Edwin looked shell-shocked.

"Sir Henry. He's a very handsome cat. I'd love to meet the others sometime."

Edwin blushed, thinking she had meant he was handsome instead. He felt silly for thinking anyone would feel that way about him.

"They're over at the office napping right now," he said absently. He dared a look at Marta's face and saw a sadness in her smile. When she returned his gaze, she could see the concern on his face.

"I had two cats of my own—Chloe and Mitzie. They were from the same litter, and I had gotten them as kittens. They were such great company for me . . ." Marta's voice broke as a tear escaped down her cheek.

"Were?" Edwin hedged.

"I recently lost them in an apartment fire. I wasn't home when it happened, and the firefighters didn't know they were in there. I can't imagine how scared my poor babies were . . ." Her voice cracked and she tried to rein in her grief, her chin quivering as she swiped the tears away.

"I'm so sorry," Edwin said softly. "I can't imagine—" They sat in silence for a moment. "But thank goodness you weren't hurt. Had you lived there long?"

Marta took a deep breath, hoping her voice would work again. "About fifteen years. I lived above the flower shop, where I work."

"You own a flower shop?"

"No, I just work there. I really enjoy it. I love plants and flowers, and I love seeing how happy they make people."

Edwin smiled, amazed at just how much he and Marta had in common—flowers, cats, Agatha Christie. His stomach did a little flip when she reached forward again to pick Sir Henry up, gathering him up in her arms and burying her nose in his soft fur. He wasn't sure what it was about her. All he knew was that he wanted to know more.

Marta's kitty snuggle was interrupted by the beeping of the washing machine cycles ending, so she put Sir Henry back down on the ground and stood. "I've got to get back to the laundry before her highness's shirts wrinkle," she said sarcastically.

"Her highness?" Edwin remembered another 'highness' comment earlier in the week.

Marta rolled her eyes. "My sister, Elaina. She was the only person I could turn to when my apartment burned down, and she and William took me in and invited me to come along on their vacation."

"Well, that was nice of them."

Marta snorted, which Edwin found incredibly endearing. "One would think. However, I'm here serving as Cinderella to earn my keep."

He looked at her with his head cocked to one side.

"I'm stuck doing all the cooking, cleaning, and laundry so that they don't have to lift a finger, as payment for them taking me in."

"That's terrible! How could someone treat their sister that way?"

"We've never been close. She's twelve years my senior, and our father favored her over me. She got everything she ever asked for. I just learned early to keep my mouth shut and live with what I had."

"What about your mom?"

Marta looked down at the ground and kicked at the dirt with the toe of her shoe. "My mom died giving birth to me," she murmured.

"I'm so sorry," Edwin said, wishing he hadn't pried.

"It's okay. I've never known what it's like to have a mother, so I don't miss her," she shrugged. "I think my dad always blamed me for my mother's death. After my sister graduated from high school and moved away, I was forced to take on the role of homemaker, doing all of the cooking, cleaning . . . not so different from right now, I guess," she said wistfully. "Anyway, I better get back to the laundry. It was really nice talking with you, Edwin," she said, smiling sweetly at him.

As she turned to walk back to the laundry cabin, Edwin began to panic. He realized he didn't want his time with her to end.

"Marta?"

She turned back to him.

"If you'd like to stop by the office sometime, I'd love for you to meet Miss Marple and Hercule," he said, stuffing his hands in his pockets and rocking back on his heels.

Marta smiled. "I'd like that, Edwin," and she walked away.

A few days later, Marta decided to borrow Elaina's car to go to the supermarket for more groceries. Elaina grudgingly gave her the keys along with several warnings about not damaging the car or parking too close to other vehicles. As Marta set out, she realized she was unfamiliar with the area and needed directions to the nearest store. She also had finished both of the books she had brought with her, and wondered if there was a library nearby. Figuring that Edwin would have the answers to her questions, she decided to stop by the office.

Walking into the tidy and well-kept office, she immediately liked its woodsy feel, like a log cabin. The décor was quaint, with furnishings depicting pine trees, moose, and bears. At the check-in desk was a small bell, which she assumed she should ring since she couldn't see or hear Edwin anywhere nearby. Her hand was poised above the top of the bell when footsteps echoed from a small room behind the desk. Edwin's head popped around the corner and he swallowed hard.

"Marta."

"Hello, Edwin. How are you?"

"Uh . . . fine. Uh . . . what can I do for you?"

"I need to go into town for some groceries, but I'm not sure where I'm going. Could you provide me with some directions please?

Edwin stepped from the office to behind the desk. "Uh . . . yes. If you go out to the main road and take a left, there's a Piggly Wiggly about five miles down the road."

"Great. That will work just fine. Thank you, Edwin," she smiled. They stood there awkwardly for a moment, neither knowing what to say. Surprisingly, Edwin broke the silence first.

"I, uh, thought maybe you were here to meet the cats."

"Oh yes! Miss Marple and Hercule. I'd love to meet them," she said, a huge smile covering her face.

Edwin mirrored her smile, and Marta's heart skipped a beat. It was the first genuine smile he'd ever given her, and it was a heartwarming sight. She found him to be really quite handsome in his own unique way. Edwin gestured for her to come behind the desk, and she followed him into the tiny office. There, curled up in an overstuffed chair, was a very chubby, but beautiful, black and white cat snuggled up to an orange-striped tabby, who lifted his head to see who dared disturb his slumber. Edwin reached down to scratch the tabby's head.

"This is Hercule, and *that* giant fluff-ball is Miss Marple," he said, gesturing toward the black and white cat.

"Ohhhh," Marta cooed. "They're just beautiful," she said as she approached the chair. She cautiously put her hand out for them to sniff and, upon seeing no fear in their eyes, she reached out to pet Miss Marple. Her fur was thick and silky soft, and she rolled onto her back, showing her furry tummy and stretching a front leg out toward Marta in invitation. Marta giggled.

"I think she likes you," Edwin said, realizing his statement held another truth.

"I think she does, too," Marta said, looking up and locking eyes with Edwin. They held each other's gaze for a long moment, both realizing the deeper meaning of their words while they each were petting the cats. Marta blushed and was the first to look away, a small smile gracing her lips. "I should probably go get those groceries."

"Sure," Edwin said resignedly. He gestured toward the office door, allowing Marta to lead the way. He held the main cabin door open for her, his hand instinctively touching the small of her back in a gesture of guidance. Marta felt a warm current run up her spine, causing her to break out in goosebumps in the warm summer heat. Edwin removed his hand as soon as he realized the personal gesture. He walked her to her car and opened her door for her.

"So left at the main road and about five miles, right?"

"That's right," he replied, closing her door for her.

"Oh, I was also going to ask if there's a library nearby."

"Library? Yes, about four blocks this side of the grocery store."

"Great. I finished the books I brought with me, and since we're still going to be here for a few weeks, I'll go crazy if I don't find something else to read. I thought maybe they'd give me a temporary library card."

I'm sure they would," Edwin replied. "But if it's books you're looking for, I have a huge collection. You're welcome to borrow anything you like."

Marta smiled. "That's right, you have all the Agatha Christies, don't you?"

"I do," Edwin said proudly.

"Well, I might have to take you up on that."

Edwin smiled and nodded. "Come by anytime."

"Thank you. Well, I'm off."

"Drive carefully, Marta."

She smiled sweetly at him and drove away.

Chapter 5

The next morning, after Marta had finished her drudgery, she decided to take Edwin up on his book offer. As she walked toward the main office, butterflies fluttered in her stomach. Surprised at how anxious she was to see the very sweet Edwin again, she wished that he wasn't so shy.

As she approached the steps that led to the office, she stopped short when she heard Edwin trying to calm a guest.

"I'm very sorry, Herb. Now please, calm down and tell me what's missing."

"Well, my grandson keeps his motorbike here so he can use it when he visits. Now, it was outside leanin' against the cabin yesterday afternoon, and when I went to let the dog out before bed last night, I saw it was missin.'"

"That's terrible. And you didn't hear anything strange during the afternoon or evening?"

"No sir! Saw it last just before you come over with the weed whacker. Must've gone missin' sometime after that."

"You know, I do remember seeing it while I was there. Bright red, wasn't it?"

"Yes, sir."

"And you don't think your grandson stopped by to get it?"

"No sir, he lives a couple states away. And even if he had been here to get it, he'd surely have let us know he was here."

"Well, I will do some investigating, Herb. We will get to the bottom of this, I assure you. I will ask the residents and guests if they've seen anything as well. I know these woods like the back of my hand, and if it's been ditched anywhere, I'll find it. You'll let me know if you hear anything as well."

Herbert blustered a bit more before turning to leave. "Humph . . ." The screen door to the cabin swung open with force, nearly knocking Marta over as Herbert stomped down the steps and hobbled back toward his cabin. Edwin stood just inside the door, a scowl marring his face as he rubbed his forehead. He didn't even notice Marta until she moved to walk away.

"Marta?"

"Hi, Edwin. I can see you're busy. I'll come back later."

"No!" His voice sounded more desperate than he had intended. "I mean, now is fine. What can I do for you?" Edwin's voice and face softened as he smiled shyly at Marta.

"Well, you mentioned you'd let me borrow a book or two?"

"Oh, yes! Certainly. They are in my residence at the back of the cabin here. Come on in." Edwin gallantly held the door open for Marta as she ascended the steps. Crossing the floor of the main office, he opened another door and stood aside to let her pass, following behind and closing the door. "I'm sorry if it's a bit messy in here. I haven't had a chance to tidy up today."

Marta gazed around the small living room. It was clear that a bachelor lived here. The furniture was very simple, made of mostly pine. Pictures of wildlife and what she assumed to be family members were placed carefully around the room. To the left of the room was a door which she assumed led to a bathroom. The back left corner looked to be his bedroom, and the back right, the kitchen.

"This is very cozy, Edwin." Marta smiled.

"Thank you. It's not much, but it's all I need, living alone and all."

Marta nodded and they stood in an awkward silence.

"Oh, the books are in my room. Follow me."

His room? Marta had never been in a man's room before other than her father's. The butterflies returned to her stomach and she hesitated, feeling as though she would be invading his privacy. He pushed the door to his room open and flipped on the light. Bookshelves lined three of the four walls in his room from floor to ceiling. Marta gasped when she stepped inside.

"Oh, my. You certainly do have quite a collection."

"I do," Edwin beamed. "All alphabetized, too. You're welcome to look around."

They heard the bell at the front desk ring and they both startled.

"I better get that. Take your time and choose as many as you like. I've read them all," he said with a polite smile as he turned to head back to the office.

Marta stood in the middle of Edwin's bedroom, his inner sanctum, and looked around, terribly nervous. His bed was made and his shoes neatly lined up at the end of his bed. On her way to the first wall of bookshelves, she walked past his closet, noting how precisely everything was hung. She reached out and let her hand trail across his shirts as she passed.

As she looked over the shelves, she was amazed at the book collection he had amassed. It appeared as though he had every Agatha Christie book ever written. He also had several other large collections ranging from Shakespeare to westerns. Marta was reading the back of an Agatha Christie book and held a book of Shakespeare's sonnets in her other hand when she jumped at the sound of Edwin's voice.

"Finding anything you like?" He paused apologetically. "I'm sorry. I didn't mean to scare you."

Marta smiled. "You didn't, really. My mind was just on all these books." She noted that Edwin seemed a bit frazzled. "Is everything okay?"

Edwin sighed. "I just had a guest come in and report something missing."

"I know. I heard that man talking to you when I came to the office."

"Yes, he was the first one. He and his wife are residents who live here year round. The person who rang the bell just a little while ago was a summer guest. She said some personal items were missing from her RV. I asked her if she could have just misplaced them, but she swears she didn't. I just don't know what's going on around her, but I'm sure going to do my best to find out."

"Would you like any help?"

"Oh, no. I couldn't ask you to do that. You're a guest here. I need to take care of it myself."

"Oh. Because I certainly wouldn't mind. Might be kind of fun to help solve a 'whodunit,'" Marta smiled.

Edwin chuckled. "I think someone's been reading too many mystery novels."

Marta blushed and smiled, looking down at her feet. When she looked back up at Edwin, their eyes locked and they both went from laughing and smiling to something a little more intense. For once, they held each other's gaze, unwavering. The room seemed a little warmer than it had a moment before.

"You have a great smile, Edwin."

He paused a beat before mustering up his courage. "Thank you. You have beautiful eyes."

"Thank you."

"So did you find some books to read," Edwin asked after an awkward moment.

"I did. May I borrow these two please?"

"Certainly." Edwin smiled warmly.

They walked out of his room and back toward the main office. "I really was serious about helping you find the thief responsible. I'm honestly a little bored just reading every day."

"And I'm guessing spending time with your sister and brother-in-law isn't high on your list of things to do."

"How'd you guess?" she answered wryly.

"In that case, I'd be grateful for the help. Maybe if we can try to create a timeline of events, we can figure out who was in the theft areas and question them. I think I'll engage the help of Ross as well," Edwin mused.

"Ross?"

"Ross is our security guy. He patrols a couple times a day just to make sure that the residents and guests are behaving and not getting out of control. Maybe he saw something on his rounds. At the very least, he should be part of the process when questioning people."

"Good idea. Shall we?" Marta said excitedly.

Edwin gestured toward the door to the office and opened it, letting Marta pass through first. They walked side by side on their way to Ross's cabin, chatting easily about the resort grounds. Edwin was impressed at Marta's knowledge of the local flora, knowing most of the different types of wildflowers and trees. Her face lit up with happiness as she talked about her job at the flower shop, and how she hoped one day to have a small home of her own where she could fill a large garden with wildflowers. She loved how they grew randomly, and how you never knew what different kinds of flowers or colors would grow when you planted the seeds.

"That's why I love sitting under that oak tree here at the resort. So many wildflowers around me. It's heavenly." She smiled brightly and Edwin's heart skipped a beat. She was more beautiful to him than any field of wildflowers. He wished he had the courage to tell her that

They arrived at Ross's cabin at the perfect time. He was just about to climb aboard his four-wheeler to make his late afternoon rounds.

"What can I do ya for, Ed?" Ross asked before he spat tobacco juice onto the ground at his feet.

"Well, I've had two people report thefts to me today. Herbert was in just before noon to tell me that his grandson's motorbike is missing. Then, a short time later, Miss Walker, one of the vacationing guests, came in to say that there were some personal items missing from her RV. Wondered if you had seen anything during your rounds yesterday or today."

"Can't say that I have. Everything's been pretty quiet. But I can stop by on my rounds now and talk with 'em."

"That would be great," Edwin replied. "I took statements and got the details from both of them about what is missing. If you could make some notes too, we can at least check to see if their stories stay consistent. I'm a little worried about the motorbike, but the missing jewelry and clothing could just be Miss Walker misplacing things. At any rate, let me know what you find. I'm going to head over to Herb's place now to look around outside, maybe see if I notice any footprints or anything amiss."

"Got it. I'll catch up with you after my rounds." With that, Ross revved up his four-wheeler and did a dramatic skid on his way out of his drive.

Once the dust cleared, Edwin looked at Marta. "Ready to do some PI work?"

"I am. Let's go!"

They turned and started out on the path across the resort to Herb's cabin. To Marta's pleasant surprise, she found Edwin's fingers intertwining with hers. A thrill ran through her at his touch. A worried but hopeful look graced his face when she glanced up at him, and when she smiled and lightly squeezed his hand, he visibly relaxed. Marta had never really had a boyfriend. She had dated a little bit in her twenties, but she found it to be terribly nerve-wracking, and most of the men she had dated were either so into themselves that they nearly forgot she was there, or they were only after one thing that she was not willing to give them.

Edwin and Marta took their time walking to Herbert's cabin. Edwin was enjoying the feel of Marta's hand in his. He, too, had never had a serious girlfriend, though not for lack of wanting one. He had grown up in a poor household, his father barely making ends meet. As a child, he wore hand-me-down clothes and made do with used glasses from the Salvation Army. He was called a nerd at school and had very few friends.

Most people would consider a childhood like his lonely, but it never really bothered Edwin. He had several brothers and sisters to play with and one good friend at school. He didn't go to college, rather he worked as an apprentice, of sorts, for a local handyman and learned how to fix and build just about anything.

In his early thirties, he began working at Happy Endings Resort as their handyman, and within a few years, he was promoted to manager. Edwin spent years learning his trade so that he would be able to provide a good life for himself and anyone else who came along. He always knew that, someday, if he had children, he wanted them to have an easier childhood than he did. However, life had gotten away from him. Here he was, forty-three years old, and while he had plenty of money in the bank, he had no one to share his life with and no one to provide for but himself and his cats.

When they got to Herbert's cabin, Ross was finishing up his inquiry. Herb showed them all where the motorbike had been parked and they all looked around for anything strange or out of place but found nothing out of the ordinary. Several sets of footprints were in the area and, as the men looked at their boots, they all realized they were the creators of the prints, and none of the prints appeared not to match.

"I do recall seeing the bike right here when I was trimming around the cabin," Edwin reported, "so we know it was last seen late in the afternoon."

"That's right, and it was gone by nine o'clock last night," Herb added.

"Herb, do you want to report the motorbike missing to the police? I can call them out here for you," Ross offered.

"Yeah, I guess we probably should, though it wasn't worth much."

"That's a good idea, Ross. Can you take care of that, please? I want to go over to Miss Walker's RV and see if I can help her find her things."

"Sure thing, Edwin. I'll check in with some of the neighbors around here too . . . see if anyone saw or heard anything. I'll stop by the office later."

Marta and Edwin took off in the direction of Miss Walker's RV. This time, Marta took Edwin's hand and they both smiled at each other. When they reached her RV, Edwin knocked on the door and Miss Walker came to the door. She reminded Marta a lot of her own sister—high maintenance, nose in the air, and similar taste in clothing. She stood in the doorway with her hand on her hip and an attitude to match.

"Miss Walker, I'm here to do a little investigating on your missing items. Is it okay if we come in?"

"Sure," she said in a thick New York accent. It sounded more like 'sho-ah.' "Who's the girl?"

"Oh, uh, this is my . . . friend, Marta. She's a guest here for a few weeks."

Marta put her hand out to Miss Walker in greeting. "Nice to meet you, Miss Walker."

"My pleasure, hon. Call me Rhonda. Come on in."

Marta and Edwin stepped up into the luxury RV and looked around. The RV reminded Marta of her sister as well.

"Miss . . . uh, Rhonda, can you show me where you had kept the items that are missing?" Edwin asked politely.

"Sure. The jewelry was here in this jewelry box. I'm missing my mother's diamond wedding ring, and a string of pearls." She walked over to the closet. "And in here, I'm missing two cashmere sweaters."

"And when was the last time you saw them?" Edwin asked.

"Well, the sweaters were here yesterday morning. I remember seeing them when I was looking for something to wear. The ring I saw three days ago."

"And has anyone else been in your RV in the past three days? Any visitors?"

"No, just me and my fiancé. Oh . . . and you, when you came to look at the air conditioner."

"Right. And are you sure you didn't wear the ring or pearls somewhere or didn't take your sweaters to the laundry or anything?"

"No. The sweaters were clean, and I only wear my mother's ring on special occasions. I haven't worn the ring or the necklace since we've been here."

Edwin looked through the jewelry box, moving it out of the way to look under it. Then he looked around the dresser it was on—behind it, underneath it.

"Have you looked through all the drawers to make sure it didn't fall in?"

"Yeah. I've been through everything."

Edwin looked briefly in the closet, parting the hanging clothes so that he could see the floor all the way to the back corners. Nothing.

"Would you like to file a formal report with the police?" Edwin asked.

"Yeah, okay."

"I'll have Ross, our security officer, give them a call for you."

Rhonda showed Edwin and Marta out and they headed back toward Herb's cabin to find Ross. Edwin held Marta's hand again, but she could tell his mind was elsewhere. His brow was furrowed and he seemed lost in thought.

"We'll find them," Marta said with encouragement and a squeeze of his hand. Edwin nodded skeptically.

The remainder of the afternoon was spent interviewing residents and guests, none of whom had seen anything out of the ordinary. As Edwin and Marta headed back to the main office, they passed William and Elaina out for a walk. Edwin and William gave each other guy nods, and Elaina looked curiously at their linked hands.

"Maaarta," Elaina cooed in her obnoxious way. "We were just out looking for you. It's getting on toward dinner time and Bill and I are getting hungry. Don't you think you should get to it?" she said, like a mother chastising a young child for playing before homework.

"Of course," Marta acquiesced, dropping Edwin's hand.

"Good. We're going to walk down to the lake for a bit, but we'll be back shortly for dinner," Elaina said smugly as she and William continued on.

Marta began to walk away when Edwin touched her shoulder to stop her. "Marta, wait."

She turned to him, her eyes cast downward. Edwin placed his finger under her chin and raised her head to look at him. "You don't have to ask how high when she tells you to jump. She doesn't own you."

A tear glistened in her eye. "I know, but I owe them at least this. They took me in when I had nowhere else to go. They let me tag along on their vacation. As much as I hate it, I feel like I need to do this to earn my keep. It's not much, really. I have it all planned out, a week's worth of menus at a time, so it's not difficult."

"That's not the point," Edwin argued. "It's the way they treat you, like you're their servant. It's not right, Marta. You deserve so much more."

Marta gave Edwin a weak smile and shrugged her shoulders. "I'd better get going. I'm sorry, Edwin."

Edwin gave a heavy sigh. "Okay. See you tomorrow?" He took her hand and brought it to his lips and gave it a tender kiss. Marta smiled brightly and turned to walk quickly to the RV.

Edwin smiled, giving himself a pat on the back for being brave enough to do what he had just done as he walked the path to his office.

Chapter 6

The next morning, while Marta was cooking breakfast for the three of them, Elaina came out from her small bedroom and sat at the folding dining table. She cleared her throat several times before Marta snapped out of her daze.

"Oh, sorry," she mumbled, then grabbed a cup and poured coffee for her sister. Marta set the cup on the table and Elaina gave her a disapproving look.

"So, I noticed you and that handyman yesterday," Elaina baited. Marta kept herself busy at the stove. "You like him?"

Marta stopped stirring the eggs for a moment. "He's a very nice man. And he's the resort manager, not the handyman," she corrected.

"So is that what you spend your days doing . . . hanging out with him?"

"Sometimes," Marta admitted.

"Well, I think you need to spend a little more time around here. You're slacking on your duties.

"I beg your pardon?" Marta turned on her sister.

"The bathroom needs to be cleaned . . ."

"I cleaned it yesterday from top to bottom."

"Well, you wouldn't know it," Elaina scoffed. "The mirror is full of streaks and I don't think you touched the stool." Marta turned back to the eggs and clenched her teeth in frustration.

"Fine. I'll clean it again."

"I'd like you to do a few more things today as well. The beds all need to be stripped and the bedding washed. My laundry is beginning to pile up, and I'd like you to take the car into town and get a few things for me."

Marta balled her hands at her sides into fists. Why all of a sudden was Elaina wanting all this extra work done? Was she jealous that Marta had finally found a friend?

"That's going to take me all day," muttered Marta.

Elaina snorted. "Well, it's not like you have anything better to do except poke your nose into a book."

"What I do with my time is no concern of yours!" Marta lashed out.

"Excuse me, missy. I'll thank you not to take that tone with me. We're doing you a favor, here. The least you could do is be a little grateful for a roof over your head and a beautiful place to stay for a month."

"I'm very grateful you took me in, Elaina. But I'm your sister, not your maid. The least you could do is treat me like an equal."

Elaina got dangerously close to Marta's face and poked her manicured fingernail into Marta's chest. "You will *never* be my equal," she said with a lethal venom. "Now, finish my breakfast."

Marta turned back to the stove, angry tears forming in her eyes, but she'd never give Elaina the satisfaction of letting her see her cry.

She served Elaina her breakfast, as well as William, who had just come in from his run. Having lost her appetite, she tore the bedclothes off of the beds, loaded the sheets into baskets and took all of the dirty laundry with her out the door of the RV, being sure to slam it as loudly as she could.

Marta stalked off toward the laundry cabin, her mind reeling with choice words for her sister. She was so tired of being treated like a second-rate member of the family, as she had been her whole life. When she reached the laundry, her mood soured further when she saw that all but one washer was being used. She had at least three loads to do, and at this rate, it would take her all morning. She got the first load going, grabbed the book she had brought along, and sat down at the picnic table with a huff. She had hoped she'd at least see Edwin this morning, but he was nowhere around.

Three hours later, Marta finally took the last of the laundry out of the dryer. She trekked back to the RV, made the beds and put the laundry away. Cleaning the bathroom—again—she made sure to scrub every surface. Then, she tidied up the entire RV and prepped a few things for dinner before running Elaina's errands for her. Upon her return, seeing that Elaina and William were nowhere around, she grabbed her book and went to find her favorite tree.

The day was beautiful and warm without a cloud in the sky. Marta got comfortable and soon was engrossed in her book when she felt something soft nudge her bare foot. She looked down to find Miss Marple rubbing her chin on Marta's toes. "What are you doing, little miss?" Marta giggled at the cat. Miss Marple sauntered over to stand next to Marta, pushing her furry little head into Marta's hand, looking for scratches on her ears. She happily obliged the sweet kitty who climbed into Marta's lap and curled up to take a nap. Marta smiled, feeling a touch of bittersweet. It had been a couple of weeks since she'd had a kitty in her lap, and she realized how much she missed Mitzie and Chloe.

When it was time to go and start dinner, she picked up her book and carried Miss Marple to the office. She went inside and rang the bell, but Edwin didn't answer, so she left the cat inside and returned to the RV for her evening of servitude.

The next morning, after her chores were done, she took her book and walked past the office on the way to her reading tree. She saw Edwin sitting on the steps with his cup of coffee. He smiled warmly and waved her over.

"You're a sight for sore eyes," he said as he scooted aside to make room for her to join him.

Marta smiled. "You must have been busy yesterday. I didn't see you."

"Miss me?"

"Maybe a little," she answered with a blush as she bumped his shoulder with her own.

"Coffee?" Edwin asked.

Marta wrinkled up her nose. "No, thank you. I'm a tea drinker."

"I have that too. What do you like?"

"I like a good Earl Grey or Chamomile."

The office phone began ringing and Edwin excused himself to answer it. Marta remained on the steps and Hercule joined her, winding his way around her ankles. She reached down to pet the tabby and scratch his head. Spotting some wild asters near the side of the building, she stood and walked over to them, bending down to touch their delicate petals. There were several varieties and colors littering the ground, creating a mosaic blanket. She and Hercule wandered back to the steps just as Edwin was returning with an extra cup in hand.

"Earl Grey. I hope you like it."

"Thank you, Edwin. You really didn't have to." She took a sip and smiled. "It's perfect."

"Hercule keeping you company?"

"He is. We walked over to look at the asters. They're so beautiful," Marta smiled wistfully.

Edwin returned her smile, but there was a dark storm brewing in his eyes.

"What's wrong?"

"Another theft," he muttered, shaking his head.

"Another one?"

"I just can't figure it out. There's no rhyme or reason to the thefts. A motorbike, a ring, pearls, some sweaters, and now a bunch of fishing gear."

"Did you interview any of the residents yesterday to see if anyone had seen anything?" Marta asked.

"No. I was tied up mowing and fixing things. I was actually at the trailer where this theft was yesterday. I was there fixing some leaky pipes, but I never saw any fishing gear. I guess I'll have to start canvassing the area to see if anyone knows anything."

"Correction. *We* will have to start canvassing the area," she countered with a grin.

"Right. We," he said as he took her hand and caressed it. "Shall we?"

Edwin collected their cups and brought them into his kitchen before returning to Marta. Just as they were about to start canvassing, Ross's four-wheeler came to a dusty halt in front of them.

"Edwin. I hate to tell you this, buddy, but I just had two more theft reports."

"Two? I had one just a while ago . . . some fishing equipment. Did they report it to you too?"

"Well, then we have three more thefts. I got reports of a portable generator and a golf cart."

"What on earth?" Marta questioned. "This just doesn't make sense."

"Right. Some of these are big items. It wouldn't be that easy to just wander off with them," Edwin mused. "Let me get my golf cart and we'll follow you, Ross. We need to interview guests and residents all over the resort to see if anyone has seen anything. Where were the last two thefts?"

"One was Tim Wilson, a guest on the other side of the resort, and the other was Janice Kramer."

Edwin suddenly went pale and broke out into a cold sweat.

"Edwin?" Marta grabbed his arm. "Edwin, what is it?"

He swallowed several times before answering. "I've done work in the last few days at all of those places. It's going to look like I did it."

"Edwin, that's crazy," Ross said. "You would never do that."

"Oh, Edwin. It's got to be just a strange coincidence," Marta said, trying to comfort him.

"I sure hope so. I swear to you both I didn't steal anything. I swear it," he said as he left to retrieve his golf cart.

When he returned, Marta climbed into the cart with him and they followed Ross to the camping spots neighboring all of the theft victims. Most of the people had nothing to report, and the three thought they had hit another dead end. However, one of the guests reported seeing a man in an olive green jacket leaving the area quickly on foot.

"Can you remember anything else about this person, Mr. Kent?" Ross asked.

"Well, he was wearing a John Deere hat and boots. Looked like he was headed out fishing, but he wasn't headed for the lake."

"Which direction was he headed?" Edwin asked.

"Toward the front of the resort. Never thought anything of it until you started asking questions."

"Do you recall how tall he was?"

"Hard to tell. I was in the trailer at the time, so I was up higher than he was. I wouldn't want to guess."

Ross took notes on his clipboard, including Mr. Kent's contact information. "I'll be reporting this to the police as well, Mr. Kent. They may be contacting you if they have any questions."

"No problem. Happy to help. Hope you find the culprit."

Two other residents had similar reports, noting a man carrying a heavy-looking red machine of some kind. The two women said they were walking back from the lake when they saw him. He, too, was wearing an olive green jacket with a green hat and he had gloves on. Edwin was happy that they were finally getting somewhere, but he still had a very uneasy feeling. Something just felt very out of place.

Late in the afternoon, the group returned to the office, exhausted and no closer to finding the thief other than a physical description. Still, it could be nearly anyone. Noting the time, Marta excused herself to return to the RV to begin making dinner.

"Marta?"

"Yes?"

"Do you have plans this evening?" Edwin asked nervously.

"I was just going to spend the evening in my bunk reading like I always do. Beats trying to make small talk with Elaina and William."

"Would you like to come back after dinner? I made an apple pie early this morning . . ." he trailed off.

"Edwin, I'd love to," she smiled brightly. "Can I bring anything?"

"Just your pretty face," he said with a shy smile.

"I'll be here," she replied before she scurried off.

Edwin went inside to prepare his own dinner, still troubled by the thefts around the resort. He hoped that he and Ross could find the culprit before having to open up a giant, ugly police investigation. So far, the dollar value of the items missing wasn't in the felony range, so he knew the thefts wouldn't be high on the police department's radar.

Edwin also hoped not to have to involve Rory, the resort's owner. He prided himself on being an excellent resort manager, and up until now, there had never been an issue or problem that Edwin couldn't handle. He knew that Rory trusted him, and he certainly didn't want to let her down. He loved his job and didn't want to do anything to jeopardize it. Eating his dinner in a daze, his mind desperately tried to put all the pieces of this puzzle together. But there was one big piece missing. He knew it . . . and he had a bad feeling about it.

Chapter 7

Marta rushed back to the RV to start dinner. She was happier than she'd been in a long time, and the thought of spending the evening with Edwin made her smile. However, her smile was short-lived when she saw Elaina scowling at her as she arrived. Elaina was sitting in her lounge chair, sipping on her gin and tonic, a sour look on her face.

"A little late today, aren't you?" Elaina chastised.

"Sorry. We were busy. The chicken is marinating. I just need to cook it and the vegetables. I'll get right on it." Marta quickly ascended the three steps of the RV and began cooking. Elaina followed a few moments later, her shoulder bouncing off of the doorway as she stumbled in, and Marta deduced that Elaina wasn't on her first gin and tonic.

"*We* were busy? Who's *we*? Were you with the handyman again?" she said with obvious distaste.

"I told you, he's not a handyman. He's the resort manager. And yes, I was helping him out with something."

"Oooohhh ... too lazy to do his own job, huh?" Elaina judged.

Marta used all of her self-control not to point the butcher knife in her hand at her sister. "Not at all. Edwin is a very busy man. He's anything but lazy." Marta wasn't sure how much she should tell her sister. She didn't want her butting her nose into Marta's business or making trouble in the theft investigation.

Elaina sat heavily onto the couch and took a large sip of her drink. William appeared behind Marta, having come from the bedroom.

"How was your nap?" Elaina cooed sloppily.

"Great," he drawled, stretching and yawning as he slipped past Marta. "I'm starved. Dinner ready yet?"

"No," Elaina groused. "Marta was late starting it. Lord knows how long we'll have to wait."

Marta turned, glaring pointedly at her sister. "Dinner will be ready in about ten minutes. Why don't you two relax outside so that I can pull the table down and get it set?"

William took Elaina's hand and helped her up, steadying her on her feet. She handed her glass to him on her way out the door. "Fix me another, Bill, will you?"

He nodded at her and got to work on her drink. He watched Marta as she rushed busily around the tiny kitchen. "What? Got a hot date tonight?" he teased.

"I beg your pardon?" Marta said, taking offense.

William held his hands up in surrender. "You just seem to be in a hurry tonight. We're not going to die in the next ten minutes if we don't eat."

"Sorry. I have plans later."

"Plans? You?"

Jenn Braddock

Marta turned on him. "Yes, William. Me. Contrary to popular belief, I'm not the social outcast you and Elaina make me out to be. I do have a life . . . a very happy one most of the time. I may not live a lavish life like you do, but I'm happy with what I have." She turned her attention back to the chicken as she flipped it on the indoor grill and stirred the vegetables in the sauté pan, effectively dismissing William and any further conversation.

A few minutes later, she called them inside to eat, avoiding any and all conversation with them. She ate her dinner quietly, listening disinterestedly at the continuing conversation they had started outside.

"So how much do you think we'd be able to get for the house?" Elaina asked her husband.

"I'm not sure. I'd have to check with the realtor. We'd have to put it at the top of the market with that second mortgage on it. I'm just afraid that, even at those prices, we would still owe money on it. We may have to sell some other things too."

"Like what?"

"Well, a couple of your cars for starters. We won't need more than two cars anyway."

"Well, you're not selling my convertible," Elaina slurred. "That's my favorite car and I won't part with it."

"Let's not worry about all that just yet. It's not like we can afford to completely retire. For one thing, we're too young to collect Social Security. If we do this at all, we'd have to look at it as semi-retirement. We'd still have to work part of the time."

Elaina pouted at her husband. "But I don't want to work anymore. We're rich, Bill. We should be able to just retire and life the high life down here. We could build a nice cabin and live here year round"

"Yes, rich . . . and in debt to our eyeballs. We have a lot to pay off before we can relax and enjoy it, El."

Marta rolled her eyes as she stood to bring her plate to the sink. She didn't understand the mindset of making all that money and then spending so far beyond one's means that you ended up owing more than you made. She was glad that, despite her rocky relationship with her dad growing up, he had at least taught her the value of a dollar and how important savings and retirement planning were. Marta would never have to worry about what she would live on when she was ready to retire. She had been careful to make wise choices.

When William and Elaina were finished eating, Marta quickly did the dishes and cleaned up the kitchen area. Then she went into the bathroom to brush her hair and fix her ponytail. Looking into the mirror, the harsh lighting made her look pale and washed out. She spied Elaina's makeup bag sitting on the small vanity and took out one of her compacts. Inside, Marta found a lovely pink blush, and added just a touch to her cheeks. Then, she applied a small amount of mascara to her lashes, making her bright blue eyes pop. Finally, she brushed her teeth and then applied a dab of clear lip gloss to her full lips. Marta gazed at her reflection, happy with the way her features were enhanced, but not overdone.

Feeling a slight chill in the air coming through the windows, she decided to change from her summer top into a lightweight, short-sleeved sweater. She just hoped that she could get out of the RV and past her sister without too much drama.

"Where are you off to?" Elaina sneered.

"I'll be back later. Don't wait up," Marta commented before turning on her heel and setting off for Edwin's in the hazy, summer dusk. She could feel Elaina's loathing gaze on her back as she walked away, a small triumph in each step she took.

Marta walked up the steps to the office. Edwin must have heard her, because she heard him calling from his quarters.

"Marta?"

"Yes, I'm here."

"Come on back. I'll be right with you."

She entered his living area and stood nervously, looking around the small but tidy room. It was comfortable and homey, and it reminded her a lot of her old apartment. As she looked around, she thought about all of the things that she would have to replace. Fortunately, she didn't have anything of any real value or sentimentality. Her father had given anything of value to her sister, so it wasn't too heartbreaking having to replace her things. The two things she had loved most in the world had been Chloe and Mitzie, and they were irreplaceable.

Edwin finally came into the room carrying a serving tray. On it sat two pieces of apple pie, and two cups—one with coffee and one with tea—and in the center was a tiny bud vase holding a few of the little asters she had seen earlier in the day. She gave him a warm smile as he set the tray down on the coffee table.

"I found a nice apple cinnamon tea in the cupboard. I hope you like it," Edwin noted.

They sat on the couch and ate their pie while listening to some beautiful classical guitar music. It was relaxing, and the pie and the tea were delicious. Edwin told her about how he grew up, about his siblings, and how he had lost both of his parents to cancer two decades ago. Marta told him about how she came to work at the flower shop and he marveled at her extensive knowledge of flowers and plants of all kinds.

Edwin was surprised to find that he was less and less nervous around Marta each time they were together, which made him happy. He was truly beginning to have strong feelings for this beautiful creature, and he didn't want to make a mess of things by fumbling around and being nervous. He reached out and plucked a yellow aster from the bud vase and handed it to Marta. She smiled and her blue eyes twinkled in the soft light of the room.

"Marta . . ." Edwin began, "would it be too forward of me to ask if I could kiss you?"

Marta's heart fluttered, but not from nerves. She, too, was finding her confidence with Edwin, and had hoped the evening might come to this. She had never felt about anyone the way she was feeling about Edwin, and the thought of him kissing her made her warm and tingly.

"Not at all," she blushed as she looked down at her flower.

Edwin brought his hand to her cheek, running his thumb across her delicate cheekbone so lightly it felt like a feather tickling her.

"Your hair is such a beautiful color. May I?" he asked, motioning to her hair tie. Marta's eyes slowly closed as she nodded, and she reveled in the feeling of the hair tie being pulled gently from her locks. Her blonde hair fell around her shoulders and Edwin gently ran his fingers over it. "So soft," he whispered.

Marta's eyes opened and they began to lean toward each other. Their lips touched in a gentle kiss, and after a moment, they both pulled away just a fraction, his eyes searching hers, seeing in them what he felt in his heart. He brought his hand up and placed it gently on the back of her neck, his fingers lightly threading through her golden tresses. He brought his lips to hers once more, opening slightly, and she responded in kind. Marta placed her hand on his knee and they kissed a while longer. Edwin tentatively traced her bottom lip with his tongue, and she tasted like apple. While their tongues danced gently together, Marta brought her hand up to Edwin's cheek, feeling the slight stubble against her palm. His skin was warm and he smelled of the outdoors.

He eventually broke the kiss, touching his forehead to hers, his heart beating hard against his chest. Marta was trying to regain her breath, and her body was flooded with sensations that were so new and wonderful. They held each other there for a moment before either of them could speak.

"Thank you for a wonderful evening, Edwin," Marta whispered.

He smiled at her and took her hand. "I wish you didn't have to go."

"Me too, but I really should get back," she smiled.

Edwin took the flower from her hand and tucked it behind her ear, smoothing out her silky hair. "I'll walk you back."

They walked into the main office, hand in hand, and as they got to the door, Marta saw a picture on the wall she had not noticed before. It resembled her reading spot in the woods, a giant oak tree and wildflowers all around. She smiled as she stepped forward to get a better look.

"We had an artist staying here one summer," Edwin began. "Loved that very spot you like to read in, so he painted it and gave it to the owners as a gift."

"It's beautiful," Marta breathed.

Turning toward the door, she noticed several jackets and hats hanging from the hooks near the door. However, two items in particular caught her attention—an olive green jacket and a John Deere hat. Marta's heart sank and she felt sick to her stomach. She tried her best not to let her discomfort show as Edwin walked her back to the RV.

"Goodnight, Marta," Edwin said and they shared one more kiss.

Inside the RV, Marta got ready for bed and climbed into her bunk. Tears fell down her cheeks, and it all made sense. The common denominator in all of the theft reports was Edwin. He had been at each and every place on the days that the items had gone missing.

Her stomach began to betray her and she fought to keep the nausea in check. The person she had begun to think was the man of her dreams was actually a thief.

Chapter 8

The next morning, Marta was up bright and early as usual, but her heart was heavy. She fought back tears as she made breakfast for Elaina and William. As they sat down to eat, Marta just picked at her plate.

"How was your evening, Marta?" Elaina asked.

Marta's eyes stung and she swallowed the lump in her throat. "Fine, thanks."

"You don't look very happy this morning. Lover boy not want you?"

Marta's head snapped up and she glared at her sister. "That's none of your business," she retorted.

"Oooh, touchy!" Elaina snickered, rolling her eyes as she shoved another forkful of eggs into her trap. "Well, I need you to pick my dress up at the cleaners today. William and I are going out this evening, so I guess the maid gets a night off," her voice dripping with sarcasm.

That was fine with Marta. She was tired of cooking for these two ingrates every night, and would welcome some time alone. Marta couldn't face Edwin today, so she would take her time going to town and, as distasteful as the thought was of spending any more time with Elaina than necessary, she decided she would stick around the RV today to try to avoid him.

Marta managed to find enough small things to do to while away most of the morning. Shortly after noon, Marta took the car and headed for the dry cleaners. As she was nearing the entrance to the resort, she saw two squad cars parked with their lights flashing, and a police officer was leading Edwin out of the office in handcuffs. She stopped the car and watched in disbelief as they loaded him into the back seat. Marta noticed Ross standing nearby, speaking to one of the officers. She turned off the car, got out, and ran over to Ross.

"Ross, what's going on? Why is Edwin in handcuffs?" She knew the answer, but she didn't want to believe it. It couldn't be Edwin. It just couldn't. Had he just played her all this time hoping to help cover up his crimes?

"Looks like we found our thief," Ross said, pain and disappointment in his voice.

"But that's impossible. How—"

"I was doing some routine checks this morning on my security rounds," Ross interrupted. "I've stepped up my patrols since the thefts started. When I came around the trailer storage building at the far side of the resort, I noticed some fresh tracks. Looked to be from a motorcycle or something. Found a bunch of fresh boot prints as well. Opened up the building and, lo and behold, found all of the missing items."

"Okay, but how does that prove that Edwin did it?"

"Well, when I went to the office to tell Edwin that I'd found the missing items, he was just hanging up his jacket. His olive green jacket."

"Okay, but that still doesn't prove anything . . ."

"He was also wearing a John Deere hat, and there was fresh mud on the jacket. Who else could it be? So rather than tell him about my discovery, I pretended I had a phone call coming in on my cell, and I left. That's when I called the cops."

"Why would he do this? What did he have to gain from a few petty thefts?" Marta wondered aloud.

"Beats me. That's for the cops to figure out. I did my job."

Marta walked back to the car in sheer disbelief. None of this made any sense, but Edwin did look guilty. She turned around to watch the police cruiser drive away with Edwin's panicked face looking at her pleadingly, and the tears she had been fighting back all morning escaped down her cheeks. She was devastated and ashamed that she had let herself fall for someone like that. Marta had dealt with so many losses in the past few weeks, she wasn't sure how much more she could take.

Marta was never so glad to be alone as she was when Elaina and William left for dinner that night. She reheated some leftovers for herself, forcing herself to eat at least a little bit before retiring to her bunk. Even reading held no interest for her tonight. She laid there thinking about Edwin and what possible motive he could have had for doing such a thing. It just didn't add up. What did it matter, really? With only five days left at the resort, she'd never see Edwin again. The reality of it all hurt, but she knew she couldn't be with someone whom she couldn't trust. The tears began to flow, and eventually, Marta cried herself to sleep.

Hours later, Marta awoke to the sounds of stumbling, dropping of keys, and shushing by her drunken sister and equally as drunk brother-in-law. Marta pretended to be asleep. The last thing she needed was to have a run-in with Elaina.

"I can't believe how well our plan worked!" Elaina whispered loudly.

"Keep your voice down!" William whispered just as loudly.

"It all worked just as we planned it. He'll get fired and you can move in for the kill."

"Shhh . . . she'll hear you."

"Oh, she's dead to the world up there," Elaina whispered.

"Come on, let's go to bed. We'll see how it all shakes down tomorrow."

Marta laid in her bunk, confused. Who were they talking about? What plan? It must be someone Bill worked with at the hotel. He was always trying to worm his way up the ladder, and it would be just like him to get someone fired in order to take their job. Honestly, Marta couldn't wait to get back to Charleston and get away from these pampered assholes.

A sharp ray of sunlight pierced Marta's eyelids when morning came. With a groan, she got out of bed and started the coffee, making herself a cup of tea in the process. She was about to start making breakfast when Elaina came stumbling out of the bedroom toward the bathroom.

"Please, no breakfast this morning. I have such a hangover. I'm going back to bed."

That was fine with Marta. Nibbling on some fruit and half of an English muffin, she finished her tea. Not wanting to spend the morning listening to the two of them snoring, she grabbed the laundry bin and headed for the door. William and Elaina were so drunk when they got back the night before, they had apparently disrobed from the door all the way to the bedroom. Annoyed, Marta gathered up the trail of discarded clothing.

When she bent down to pick Williams dress shirt, the cuff was caught on the handle to a small cubby under one of the benches. Giving it a slight tug, the cubby door dropped open and some kind of fabric billowed out from the opening. She reached to stuff it back in when she noticed the color.

Olive green.

Suddenly, the conversation she had overheard last night popped into her mind. She slowly pulled the item out of the compartment and found it was a jacket nearly identical to the one Edwin had. Curious now, she knelt down on the floor and reached inside the cubby once more. Tears stung her eyes when her fingers touched it. Praying she was right, she slowly pulled the item out. It was all starting to make sense.

Marta stuffed the items back into the little compartment, grabbed the laundry and scurried off as quietly as she could to find Ross. He was just getting onto his four-wheeler when she ran up to him, breathless.

"Ross . . . wasn't Edwin . . . call police . . ."

"Whoa, slow down there. What's this all about?"

Marta caught her breath as quickly as she could and continued. "Ross, I don't think Edwin did it. It just doesn't make sense. He has no motive."

"Marta, I don't understand it either, but the evidence doesn't lie. Just because we don't want it to be true doesn't make it so."

"Ross, listen. I was gathering up laundry in the RV this morning and I found the evidence. I found an olive green jacket and a John Deere hat stuffed into a cubby under a bench in the RV."

Ross looked at her quizzically, but shook his head. "It's not a crime to own a jacket and a hat."

"Tell that to Edwin," Marta said angrily, and Ross nodded resignedly. "I also heard Elaina and William talking when they came in late last night. They thought I was asleep. They were saying something like 'our plan worked' and 'he'll get fired and you can go in for the kill.'"

"Okay, but why in the world would your sister and her husband want Edwin fired? What do they care? They have more money than God. What do they want with someone like Edwin?"

Marta pondered his question. He had a good point. Edwin seemingly had nothing that they'd want. It wasn't like he owned the place or anything. He was just the resort manag—

"That's it!"

"What's it?" Ross asked, confused.

"The other night at dinner, William and Elaina were talking, and I was mostly ignoring them, as usual. They were talking about retiring early and that they wanted to retire down here, but they are in debt to the rafters and would have to sell their house and cars and work at least part time to be able to do it."

"Yeah, so?"

"So William is the general manager of one of the biggest hotel chains in South Carolina."

"I'm still not following you."

"Endings, South Carolina, is a small town, Ross. There are no big hotels here and the closest ones are back in Charleston where they live now. They want to retire down here but can't afford it. William has weaseled his way up the corporate ladder his whole life. He doesn't know how to do anything else. Ross . . . William wants Edwin's job."

Marta watched as the proverbial lightbulb went off over Ross's head. Was it possible that William and Elaina had set Edwin up to get fired so that William could try to move into Edwin's job?

"I see where you're coming from, but it sounds pretty far-fetched, don't you think?"

"Ross, it's at least worth looking into. I put the jacket and hat back where I found them. Let's tell the police about it and have them come out to search the RV. If they think you've got a strong lead, they'll come out here. You're the head of security here. Please," Marta pleaded.

"You do realize this is your sister and brother-in-law we're talking about here. Your flesh and blood. You'd rather see them go down for this than a guy you've just met?"

"Ross, Elaina has never been a sister to me. She was an over-privileged, pampered, spoiled brat as a kid . . . and she still is. She and Bill treat me like crap. I've had to work for everything I have while she's had her life handed to her on a silver platter. They'll do anything they have to in order to get their way. They're guilty. I know it."

Ross nodded in understanding and took out his cell phone. Within minutes, the police were on their way and Ross and Marta sat on the four-wheeler to wait.

"You love him, don't you?" Ross asked.

"Who?"

"Edwin."

Marta thought about his question for a long moment. Was she in love with Edwin? He made her stomach feel funny and her heart flutter. They had a great deal in common and she enjoyed his company. In all honesty, she could see herself growing old with him. And the thought of being without him made her heart hurt.

Can someone fall in love in a few short weeks? "I think I do," Marta said.

Ross called the police and explained the situation to them. The detective was skeptical, but said he would at least get a warrant and search the RV. When the detective arrived at the resort, Marta told him where to find the jacket and the hat, and once the detective was done searching, he had also recovered muddy boots and a pair of black work gloves. The boots matched the prints found at the crime scenes and the storage building, and the gloves had flecks of red paint imbedded in the fibers. Soon, Elaina and William were being led out of the RV in handcuffs, and Elaina aimed her venomous tongue at Marta.

"You bitch! Who do you think you are? How could you do this to me? I'm your sister!"

"Oh, so now you decide to feel some loyalty?" Marta spat back. "You've never once treated me like your sister. I've always been a second-class citizen in your eyes, and, oh, yes . . . wasn't it you who said I would never be your equal? Well, dear sister, you've shown your true colors, and I wouldn't want to be your equal . . . and you'll *never* be mine."

Elaina glared at Marta as her words were thrown back at her. As she was placed in the back of the police cruiser, Marta looked at the detective. "So what now?"

"Well, we take these two in and get their statements, process the evidence. We found a piece of fabric on one of the fishing lures, looks to be like the jacket material. The jacket we just recovered has a tear in it and a piece missing. Edwin's jacket is intact. I think it's a pretty open and shut case. Not only will they be charged with the thefts, but they'll also be slapped with a host of other charges related to what they tried to do to Edwin."

"And Edwin? What happens with him?"

"As soon as we get these two processed and are sure that he's in the clear, he'll be released. Could be a few days though."

"I see," Marta said, sadly. "Thank you, officer."

After they drove away, Ross looked at Marta. Marta had truly never felt as lost as she did right at that moment. Without a word, she walked away and headed back to the RV. She had no idea what she would do now. She needed to get back to Charleston and her job and find a way to get her life back in order. After pondering it for a few hours, she decided that she'd take Elaina's car and go back to Charleston. She'd leave the RV at the resort to be impounded and hauled away. No way would she'd be able to drive that huge thing herself, and she wouldn't know what to do with it once she got home anyway.

The detective said that it might be a few days before Edwin would be released. Marta wasn't sure if she should wait or go back home. She didn't know if she could face Edwin. She lost faith in him when the chips were down, and for that, she truly felt ashamed. Marta had known in her heart that he couldn't have done those things, but she had let her head believe it. So, she decided she would head for home the following day and leave Edwin and Happy Endings Resort behind for good. He deserved better.

Chapter 9

Marta barely slept at all that night, and when she woke, she had one thing on her mind. Going home. After a light breakfast, Marta gathered up what few belongings she had brought with her and put them in the car. Taking one last walk through the RV, she grabbed the keys off the counter and was about to walk out the door when she remembered the books she had borrowed from Edwin. She reached into her sling bag and pulled them out, deciding to give them to Ross to return for her. She locked up the RV and drove Elaina's car to Ross's cabin, but didn't find him there. She hoped that he'd see him on the way out. If nothing else, she'd mail the books to Edwin.

As she neared the office, she saw Ross working on his four-wheeler. Grabbing the books, she got out of the car and approached him.

"You leavin'?" Ross asked, eyebrows raised.

"Yeah. I need to get back home . . . see how my apartment is coming along . . . return to work."

"Sure. You gotta do what you gotta do."

Marta thought Ross almost seemed angry or disappointed with her, but she couldn't understand why.

"Are you okay, Ross?" Marta questioned.

"Yup," he said with a clipped tone.

"Um, would you mind giving these books back to Edwin for me when he comes back please? I borrowed them while I was here and I wanted to be sure he got them back."

"I'm all greasy here. Go put them inside the office on the desk. He'll find them. Door's open."

"Oh, okay," she mumbled.

Marta walked up the steps and opened the door into the office. The room smelled familiar. Like Edwin. She knew how much she would miss this place, and him, but there was no use in staying. She'd never forgive herself for not believing in him. She certainly couldn't expect his forgiveness.

She set the books on the desk and heard a small sound. She looked down to see Hercule and Miss Marple at her feet, and she smiled. "Goodbye, you two. You take good care of each other, okay? And take good care of Edwin for me, got it?" She gave them each a pat on the head and she stood and walked to the door.

"Aren't you going to say goodbye to me?"

Marta stopped dead in her tracks. Tears sprang to her eyes and she slowly turned around. Edwin stood behind the desk and Marta's heart nearly exploded when she saw the pain etched in his face. He looked so forlorn standing there. She wanted to run to him and throw her arms around him, but she couldn't. She had betrayed him, and her shame kept her rooted to her spot.

"Edwin, I—"

"You're just leaving?"

"I need to get back to Charleston. My apartment should be almost finished, and I have my job, and—"

"I see," his expression sad.

"Edwin, I'm so sorry . . . for everything that happened . . . for not believing in you. I hope someday you can forgive me."

"Forgive you?" Edwin said incredulously, causing Marta to wince, afraid of what was coming next. "Marta, there's nothing to forgive. When they released me today, the detective said that William and Elaina had been planning this for a long time. Last summer when they were here, William apparently studied me quite a bit, all the way down to the kind of jacket and hat I wore. He wanted it to look like it was me committing the thefts, and apparently it worked. Right up until the point that you put all the clues together when you found his jacket. You didn't do anything wrong. Marta, you saved my life. You turned in your own flesh and blood to prove my innocence."

"But I failed you, Edwin. I let myself believe you were guilty even though I knew in my heart you weren't. I should have fought for you."

"But you did fight for me, Marta. Don't you see? No one has ever done anything like that for me. Ever. Now I'd like to return the favor."

Marta was confused. "What?"

"You say you need to go back to Charleston, but for what? Your job? You lost your apartment, your cats, your sister. You can work in a flower shop anywhere, if that's what you really want to do. Marta, before you came into my life four weeks ago, I would go through the same routines day in and day out. I was existing. But then I met you and my life began to have meaning. I started looking forward to getting up every morning knowing I'd be seeing you. I could finally dare to see a future in my life. I wasn't existing anymore. I began living. Marta, I don't want to lose that. I don't want to lose you. Please don't go."

Marta's heart felt as though it would overflow as the tears spilled from her eyes. "I don't want to lose you either, Edwin."

Edwin stepped from behind the desk and walked across the room to Marta. "You once told me that you dreamed of having your own home someday where you could have a garden filled with wildflowers. And I know we've only known each other a short time, but I've never felt about anyone the way I feel about you, Marta. If you feel the same way, then please stay. Stay with me."

Marta stepped closer to Edwin and, unable to speak over the lump in her throat, she nodded and took Edwin's face in her hands and kissed him sweetly. Edwin hugged her and deepened the kiss as she wrapped her arms around his neck. When they pulled back, Marta looked into Edwin's eyes and saw what she was feeling reflected back to her.

"I love you, Edwin."

Edwin's grin lit up his face. "I love you too," he answered as he pulled her in for another kiss.

"'Bout damn time," Ross muttered from the door with a smirk.

Epilogue

By the end of the summer, William and Elaina had been charged and pleaded guilty to the thefts, which ended up being felonies when the value of everything was added up, as well as conspiracy. Their RV was impounded and sold. Marta had been right. Their plan all along had been to frame Edwin for the thefts and get him fired so that William could worm his way into Edwin's job as resort manager so they could semi-retire at Happy Endings.

"Your honor, I respectfully request that my clients be given probation in lieu of time in prison. They both have careers and will suffer great financial loss if they are subjected to the absence involved with a prison sentence."

The judge looked at the lot of them over the top of his spectacles. "Duly noted, counselor. However, I find the motives and actions of your clients truly despicable. Therefore, I am sentencing them each to five years in prison with the possibility for parole after the third year. Case closed," he replied with a bang of his gavel.

Marta did return to Charleston for a week to check on Eloise and LeRoy and to get some of her affairs in order. Eloise had been able to reopen the flower shop, and the work on Marta's apartment was near completion.

"Eloise, I have something I need to tell you."

"What is it, dear?"

"Well, while I was away this past month, I met someone." Marta couldn't stop the bright smile that was spreading across her face. "I won't be coming back to work or to my apartment."

"Well, my stars! Who is the lucky man?"

"His name is Edwin, and he manages the resort where I've been staying. We've fallen in love, and he's asked me to move in with him."

"Oh, Marta, I am so happy for you, dear. We will certainly miss you around here, but I would never stand in the way of your happiness. Promise me you'll keep in touch. And I had better see an invitation to the wedding. I'll be doing your flowers, after all."

Marta blushed. "Oh, Eloise, I don't know if or when that will be happening, but if it does, you'll be the first to know."

Eloise pulled her in for a hug. "It will happen, love. I know it will. I have a feeling about you two."

As summer turned into fall, many of the seasonal guests returned home, and the resort was quieter than normal. Marta enjoyed being with Edwin, and her moving into his small living quarters had gone seamlessly. It was as if they had lived together for years, and they were happier than they had ever been.

One evening late in the fall, as they sat reading by the fireplace, Edwin got up and went to his tiny office behind the front desk. When he returned, he sat on the heavy, log coffee table in front of Marta and held out a cardboard storage tube.

"What's this," she asked, confused.

"Open it."

She lifted the cover and slid the contents into her hand. Unrolling the paper, she stared at what appeared to be plans for a building or house of some sort. "Okay . . . what is it?"

Edwin shifted forward an inch and put his warm hands on Marta's knees. "A beautiful lady once told me about a dream she had. She wanted to have a small home with a garden where she could plant wildflowers."

Marta's head snapped up and tears filled her eyes. "Oh, Edwin, no . . ."

A warm smile spread across his face as he nodded. "For you, Marta." He leaned in and kissed Marta tenderly before Sir Henry interrupted their moment with a pang of jealousy as he walked between them, his high tail tickling their chins. They both chuckled as they broke the kiss.

"Oh, Edwin. He's got something stuck to his tail. He must have dragged something in from outside. C'mere Henry," she called.

The cat circled around and rubbed up against Marta's legs. She bent down and ran her hand along his back and up the length of his tail, and she gasped when she realized what was there. Edwin plucked the shiny object from Sir Henry's tail and gave him a pat on the head.

"Good boy, Henry," he praised.

Edwin looked at his beautiful Marta as tears welled up in her eyes and her hand covered her mouth. He gently took her left hand and held the ring at the tip of her finger.

"I love you, Marta, and I would like to spend the rest of my life making you as happy as you make me. Marry me?"

Marta nodded, swallowing over the lump in her throat as he slid the ring onto her slender finger. "Yes. Oh, yes, Edwin. You make me so happy. I love you, too."

Edwin kissed her again, long and slow before resting his forehead against hers. "If I could, I'd give you the world, Marta. But for now, I hope you'll accept me, a house with three cats and your flowers."

Marta smiled. "It's all I'll ever need, my love."

About Jenn Braddock:

I am an author of contemporary romance, as well as an editor. I live in Minnesota with my husband, two daughters, two cats and two dogs. Flowers for Marta is my first published work, and I have several other novels in the works. Please follow me on Facebook.

https://www.facebook.com/JennBraddockAuthor.